Raintree is an imprint of Capstone Global Library Limited, a company incorporated in
England and Wales having its registered office at 264 Banbury Road, Oxford, OX2 7DY
— Registered company number: 6695582

www.raintree.co.uk
myorders@raintree.co.uk

Designed by Kay Fraser
Original illustrations © Capstone Global Library Limited 2022
Originated by Capstone Global Library Ltd
Printed and bound in India

978 1 3982 3469 7

British Library Cataloguing in Publication Data
A full catalogue record for this book is available from the British Library..

SHARE THE FEAR!

You are not alone. And I don't mean that a creature lurks in the dark shadows of your bedroom. Or a slimy menace lives under your bed. (Although that might be true.) I mean, you are not alone in being afraid. Everyone is afraid of something. Every. Single. Person. Reading about other people's fears in these weird tales, you might learn how to overcome your own. Or you might learn how to escape from zombie teachers attacking the school. Both are good things to know. Just make sure you leave the lights on while reading!

CONTENTS

Chapter 1

THE SEA-CRET KEEPER

"It's just a few months, that's all," Jordan's mum said. "Your dad and I just need the summer alone to talk about things."

She tried to straighten Jordan's shirt, but he backed off and pushed her hands away. He was twelve – not a baby. He glanced around the street of the small coastal town of Cape May to see if anyone had noticed. But it was just him and his parents, standing outside his grandpa's small, run-down house.

He wasn't a baby, but Jordan already felt homesick thinking about a summer without his parents or friends – stuck in the small house with his grandpa, Captain Joe. So what if it was across from the beach. There would be no basketball games and no video games with his friends.

Jordan's dad ruffled his already messy, brown hair. "You'll have fun, Jord," he said. "Who doesn't want to be by the beach all summer? Maybe you can learn how to surf. Or Grandpa will teach you how to sail his boat. He knows a lot about the sea, you know. People used to come and ask him all of their seafaring questions."

As if they'd summoned him, Captain Joe opened the door and grunted at them. Jordan was tall for his age, but his grandpa towered over him. He wore a boat captain's hat, and grey hair poked out from the sides and back of it. He and his grandpa seemed to have messy hair in common, anyway.

"Well, don't just stand there all day," Captain Joe said. "Get inside."

They walked in and Jordan got a whiff of the house. It smelled musty and briny. Hardly any light made it inside and there were things piled everywhere.

His grandpa turned to Jordan's parents. He rubbed his white and grey, scruffy stubble. He studied them with blue, twinkly eyes. "Well, are you staying or going?"

Jordan's mum laughed. "We'll let Jordan get settled." She turned to Jordan, and he tried hard not to cry. He looked down and refused to look her in the eyes.

"It's just for a few months. We'll call you every day," his mum whispered. She wrapped him in a hug, and he tried hard not to cling on. When she had finished, his dad hugged him.

His voice was gruff. "Do as Captain Joe says. Love ya, kiddo."

Jordan mumbled, "Love you too," to both his parents.

Captain Joe hugged Jordan's mum and gave his dad a hearty handshake. "I'll look after the boy. Don't you worry," he said.

Jordan tried hard not to take that as a threat.

He watched as his parents walked out the door and abandoned him. They waved as they left, and Jordan's stomach sank.

It was real. They really were leaving him here. And he hadn't said a word to stop them.

When he turned around, his grandpa was sizing him up with one squinty eye.

"Let's go for a walk, kid. You can get to know the place," he said. He looked Jordan up and down. "I'll need to feed you more, too, to get some meat on your bones. You'll need good muscles on the boat. Pump up those skinny little legs." Captain Joe didn't wait for Jordan to follow. He just adjusted his hat and walked out the door. Jordan scrambled after him.

They walked across the street to the Cape May boardwalk. Jordan had to practically run to keep up with his grandpa. But soon he found the rhythm and was able to take in the scenery. Gulls circled overhead, squawking. The roar of the sea drowned out nearly everything else. But Jordan found he loved the sounds and the smell in the air.

A young couple walked past them on the boardwalk. Both of them nodded at his grandpa and said, "Captain." Everyone they passed, in fact, nodded and called him Captain. It seemed as if he knew the whole town.

They walked until they came to a marina where some boats were docked. Captain Joe led Jordan to a relatively small boat. It looked old but clean and sturdy. The name *The Sea-cret Keeper* was on the back. On the dock next to it was a sign that said, *Tours: $20 for one hour.*

"This is my beauty," said Captain Joe. "She's been my boat for more than thirty years now. Both she and the sea have been very good to me. If you respect things, they will respect you back."

Something shiny to the left caught Jordan's eye. A much larger, newer boat sat at the dock next to Captain Joe's. On its back end was the name *The Dream Maker.* A huge arch on the dock next to the boat had the words, *Make Your Dreams Come True!* across it. A sign tacked on the arch said, *Guided Tour and More! $50.*

Captain Joe saw where Jordan was looking and scowled. "Yeah, *The Dream Maker* looks fancy," he said. "But the owner does some pretty awful things. Fishing for endangered species. Thinking he owns the ocean. Nothing good will come of that, mark my words."

Jordan brought his gaze back to *The Sea-cret Keeper*. "What secrets does your boat keep?"

Captain Joe threw back his head and laughed. "Stick with me, kid, and I'll let you in on a few of them." His eyes twinkled and his whole face lit up.

Jordan grinned as they continued their walking tour of the harbour. Maybe this wouldn't be the worst summer after all.

Chapter 2

NEW FRIENDS

The next morning, Jordan woke to an empty house. A note left on the cluttered table said, *Cereal in cupboard. Milk in fridge. Got a tour to do – go and explore and come back for lunch. Your mum told me to tell you to put on suncream.*

Jordan couldn't believe it. His parents hardly ever let him do stuff by himself. But after he got dressed, ate breakfast and put on suncream, he wasn't sure where to start. Finally, he decided to go to the boardwalk and head in the opposite direction from which he and Captain Joe had walked the night before.

The boardwalk was busy! The temperature had spiked, and it seemed like everyone had decided to hang out at the beach. Jordan walked for about a half a mile when he spotted some basketball courts in the distance. He could see kids playing and his heart soared. He tried not to get too excited. They could be way older than him. Still, he hurried along until he was right next to the courts.

Two boys, who were obviously brothers, were playing together. Jordan thought they were probably about his age. He stood awkwardly by the courts, watching, not sure how to introduce himself. It turned out he didn't have to.

"Hey!" said one of the boys. "Want to play HORSE?"

Jordan grinned. "Yeah. I'm in!"

For the next hour-and-a-half, Jordan played hard. He couldn't stop smiling. He missed his friends, but these guys seemed cool. His new summer friends were twins called Derek and Tyler, and they were pretty good at basketball.

Jordan looked at his watch – it was almost time for lunch.

"I have to walk back to my grandpa's now," he said.

"If you're going that way, we'll walk with you," said Derek. He pointed the way Jordan had come. "Our dad's down that way. He owns *The Dream Maker.*"

They started walking, Tyler bouncing the ball every other step.

"Oh, I saw your boat!" Jordan said. "My grandpa owns *The Sea-cret Keeper*. It's right next to yours."

Derek and Tyler shared a look and snorted. "Your grandpa is Captain Joe? Are you staying with him all summer?"

Jordan wasn't sure what was so funny. "Yeah," he said uncertainly.

"Good luck with that!" Tyler said, and the twins dissolved into laughter. Jordan frowned.

Derek looked up. "Oh, sorry, man," he said. "It's just the captain is always going on about treating the sea with respect, blah blah blah. We just think he's funny, that's all. Plus his boat is so tiny."

They were almost at his grandpa's house, and Jordan slowed down. He laughed uneasily. "I don't really know him that well," he said. He stopped in front of the house.

"Well, don't worry," Tyler said. "We'll hang out with you. You can just stick with us this summer. We'll get you tomorrow, okay?"

He threw the ball at Derek and then started running down the boardwalk, bumping into people. "Over here, Derek!" he yelled.

Derek grinned and took off after him, leaving Jordan to think about his new friends.

Chapter 3

GODDESS OF THE SEA

After lunch, Captain Joe took Jordan to *The Sea-cret Keeper*. He pointed to the front of the boat. "Bow," he said. Then he pointed to the back. "Stern."

Then his grandpa pointed to the right side of the boat and said, "Starboard." Then the left, "Port." Get to know these terms – if you're going to be my first mate, you should know a thing or two."

Jordan smiled to himself. He liked the idea of being first mate. He put on his life jacket and then climbed into the boat, practising the new terms under his breath.

Captain Joe climbed in and untied the rope. He started the engine and then winked at Jordan. His whole face had changed – now he glowed with happiness. Gone was the gruff and grumpy guy he seemed to be.

"Ready?" his grandpa asked, winking again and grinning. Jordan grinned back and nodded. Captain Joe pushed the throttle, and Jordan felt the first spray of the sea.

The wind whipped through his hair as the boat sped forwards. Jordan couldn't remember feeling happier. Being on the boat felt like flying. Captain Joe pointed and shouted something that Jordan couldn't hear. But he followed the captain's finger and saw a pod of dolphins leaping in the air not too far away from them. Jordan's face hurt from smiling so much.

When they were far enough out in the sea that Jordan could barely see land, Captain Joe cut the engine.

"What do you think, kid?" he asked Jordan.

"This is awesome!" Jordan practically yelled.

Captain Joe laughed and sat down across from him. "Can't say I mind it myself," he said.

His grandpa leaned down and opened a tiny, beaten-up-looking cool bag under his seat. He grabbed a drinks can and gave it to Jordan.

"I've been sailing since I was your age," Captain Joe said. "First it was sailboats. Then I got this beaut when I was in my twenties. I've seen some things on these seas, let me tell you. Things can go south quicker than a blink of an eye. But if you pay attention and take care of the sea, she'll take care of you."

"What things have you seen?" Jordan asked. The waves rocked the boat, and the breeze blew gently against him. Jordan could still see the dolphins playing near by.

"Hmm. Let me tell you a little about the ocean here," Captain Joe said. Jordan settled back against the seat and took a sip of his drink.

"The sea is a fickle thing, and she demands respect," his grandpa continued. "Our job is to protect her – we make sure she's taken care of, and that her creatures are honoured. These new young outfits, like *The Dream Maker*, they come out here and they fish for things they have no business fishing for. I've made quite an enemy of them and others, speaking out against their practices. But the measure of a person is standing up and speaking up for what's right. Mark my words, son, if they keep up that foolishness, the sea will have its revenge."

Jordan thought about how the boys he had met laughed about Captain Joe. And Jordan hadn't said anything. He looked down and took another sip of his drink to hide his shame.

"Psst. Kid. Look over there," Captain Joe suddenly whispered.

Jordan looked to where the captain was pointing, wondering why he was whispering all of a sudden. At first he saw nothing. Then he saw a beautiful white dolphin leaping out of the water next to them, so close Jordan could almost touch her.

"It's Tia," Captain Joe said quietly. Jordan thought he saw a tear in his eye. "That's Tiamat, the goddess of the ocean. She's come to say hi!"

Captain Joe smiled broadly. He went into the engine cabin and played a special horn. The dolphin leaped and then spun in the air before splashing down.

Jordan laughed and Captain Joe whooped, being his loud self again.

"I play that horn especially for her!" his grandpa said.

"I've never seen a white dolphin before," Jordan said. "She's beautiful!" Just as the words left his lips, Tia leaped and spun again. Then she stood up on her tail. Jordan laughed with glee.

"This is a real honour. This is why we take care of the ocean. Look at that beauty," Captain Joe said.

With a flick of her tail, Tia sped towards them and leaped all around the boat. Jordan thought he might have a little tear in his eye too. He'd never seen anything so wonderful. Then, as fast as she'd come, Tia disappeared. Jordan and Captain Joe shared a look and a smile.

"Well, I think that's as good as it's going to get," Captain Joe said. "Might as well call it a day." He pushed the button to pull up the boat's anchor.

"That there was the goddess of the ocean, sure as I'm living and breathing, Jordan." Captain Joe looked him in the eye. "Legend has it when Tia is feeling good, the ocean is good. But if Tia doesn't like something, or if she's threatened . . . the other part of the ocean comes alive. And that's one part you don't ever want to meet."

"What part?" Jordan asked.

Captain Joe's eyes darkened.

"The Kraken," he said. "If Tia wants revenge, she sends the Kraken. And nothing will save you then."

His grandpa started the engine and Jordan got a chill. He didn't want to meet that part of the ocean either. He hoped he never would.

Chapter 4

NOT QUITE A DREAM

The next morning, Jordan still felt elated from the boat ride the day before. He wanted to ask his grandpa if he could join him on his tours and learn more about the ocean. But before he could, someone knocked on the door.

"I'll get it," Jordan said. Captain Joe grunted.

When Jordan opened the door, Derek and Tyler stood on the doorstep. They craned their necks to peek around Jordan and see inside the house, but he blocked their view.

"Hey," Tyler said. "We wanted to know if you could come and hang out with us today."

Jordan felt a thrill – even though he wasn't totally sure about them yet. Still, they were his age. And they liked basketball. He felt Captain Joe come up behind him.

"Derek. Tyler," Captain Joe said. "Your father doing alright, I gather?"

"Yessir," Derek said. Jordan thought he saw a little smirk.

"Can I hang out with them?" Jordan asked.

His grandpa tightened his lips. "Do what you want. Just be back for dinner," he said as he walked away, leaving Jordan uncertain in the doorway.

"Come on," Tyler said. "We're going to have fun." He and Derek turned away, and Jordan took one last look at his grandpa before shutting the door and following them.

Once they reached the boardwalk, Jordan asked, "What do you want to do today?"

"Do you want to see our boat?" Derek asked. "It's just up ahead."

Jordan perked up. "Yeah! I went out on my grandpa's boat yesterday. It was pretty awesome."

"That old thing?" Tyler said. "Wait until you see ours."

They reached the dock where *The Dream Maker* sat. Jordan once again felt impressed by how big and shiny it was. A man climbed up on deck wearing a red polo shirt and khaki trousers. He ran a hand through his glossy hair.

"You must be Joe's grandson, huh? He's quite a guy." The man shared a look with Derek and Tyler. "I'm Mr Paxton, Derek and Tyler's dad. Why don't you climb on up here to see how a real boat runs."

Jordan didn't like the way they all talked about his grandpa. But he really wanted to see what *The Dream Maker* was like. So he followed Derek and Tyler onto the deck and put on his life jacket. He and Derek and Tyler sat in some fancy bucket seats next to each other.

"You're in for a real treat, boys. If we've timed it right, you'll get to see something pretty amazing soon," Mr. Paxton said. He turned on the boat's engine, and Derek and Tyler did a high-five. Jordan smiled and high-fived them too. Maybe he should relax a bit. His grandpa did take a little getting used to, he had to admit.

The boat sped off into the waves, knocking hard against them. Jordan had to hold onto his seat so he wasn't bounced off. He couldn't believe how fast they were going. This didn't feel anything like yesterday – the wind whipped against his face and the water sprayed

up at him so hard that it stung his cheeks. Derek and Tyler seemed to be having the time of their lives, though. They laughed hysterically through the whole thing.

"Isn't this awesome?" Tyler yelled. Jordan tried to smile and nod. But he started feeling a little sick.

Finally the boat slowed down and Jordan could hear again. The engine still ran but it was low now, with the boat barely moving forwards.

"Okay, boys, keep your eyes open. We're looking for a white dolphin," Mr Paxton said as he moved towards the front of the boat – the bow, as Jordan now knew it. "I saw her a while back so I know she's here. And I also know she'll look fantastic on my mantelpiece."

"Yes!" Derek and Tyler said at the same time and moved to the sides of the boat, looking over the edges.

Jordan wasn't sure he'd heard Mr Paxton correctly. He moved over to where Tyler was leaning over.

"What did your dad say?" Jordan asked quietly.

"He's going to hunt a white dolphin! It'll go up on the wall, just like his other trophies. A great hammerhead shark. A leatherback turtle. He collects endangered species," Tyler said with excitement.

"Ahem. I 'accidentally' got those as trophies," Mr Paxton said, using his fingers to make air quotes. "Just like I'm going to *accidentally* get that white dolphin." He winked at Jordan. "Don't tell your grandpa! He gets all worked up about these things."

Now Jordan really did feel sick. Before he could say anything, Derek yelled, "Dad! Over there!"

To Jordan's horror, Tia swam just a few metres away, leaping through the water and doing her flips. Jordan knew he should say something. He couldn't let this happen.

But when he tried to speak, nothing came out of his mouth.

Mr Paxton raised a deadly looking harpoon gun and aimed it at Tia. Tia swam closer, slowing down. Jordan wanted to shout at her to SWIM AWAY! But still no words came out. Jordan's eyes filled with tears.

"Stay right there, you magnificent creature," Mr Paxton said softly. As his finger tightened on the trigger, Jordan did the only thing he could think of. He pretended to trip over right into Mr Paxton.

Mr Paxton shot the harpoon exactly when Jordan bumped into him, and it went wide. Still, Jordan watched helplessly as the harpoon

skimmed Tia, leaving a long, angry red mark on her back. Tia stopped and looked at them.

"I'm sorry," Jordan mouthed. Then Tia dived under the water.

"Damn it!" Mr Paxton said, dropping the harpoon gun. "Now she'll dive down and we won't see her again for days. Maybe not ever."

"Sorry, Mr Paxton," Jordan said – not meaning it one bit. Derek and Tyler gave him dirty looks, but Jordan felt nothing but relieved that Tia had got away.

"It's fine," Mr Paxton said, though it looked like it pained him. "There's always another day. Might as well head back since this trip has been wasted."

Jordan couldn't agree more. He wanted nothing more than to be back at his grandpa's.

Chapter 5

THE NIGHTMARE MAKER

That night, Jordan couldn't sleep. He kept replaying the scene where Tia almost got harpooned. He kept wondering why he hadn't said anything. His grandpa's words echoed in his head: *The measure of a person is standing up and speaking up for what's right.*

When he got up in the morning, he'd made up his mind. He was going to tell Mr Paxton that what he did was wrong. And he was going to tell Derek and Tyler that his grandpa was one of the coolest guys he'd ever met.

After making the decision, Jordan couldn't keep still. Sitting at the breakfast table, he kept looking at the door and fidgeting, anxious to get going and make things right.

Captain Joe eyed Jordan's bouncing knee. "You look like you have some things to say," he said.

Jordan swallowed. He couldn't summon the nerve to tell him what happened. He had to say his piece to Mr Paxton and the boys first. So he just shook his head.

The captain looked at him for a minute longer, then nodded. "Alright then," he said. "I'll be leading a tour in a while. The water is looking a little restless today. I want to get the tourists in and out before she takes a turn for the worse. Will you be joining me?"

Jordan swallowed his cereal. "Can I join you after your first run?" he asked.

"If that's what you want, son," Captain Joe replied.

Jordan nodded and got up. "I just have to do something first." He walked to the door and turned to wave at his grandpa.

"I hope you can ease whatever is troubling you," Captain Joe said.

Jordan nodded. He intended to. He stood tall and walked out the door.

Walking quickly to the boardwalk, Jordan noticed that the sea really did seem restless. The waves were rolling steadily, and the sky was turning grey. He hurried up to where *The Dream Maker* sat, hoping to see Mr Paxton and maybe the boys. Jordan glanced longingly at *The Sea-cret Keeper*, silently promising the boat he'd see her later.

Suddenly, the engine of *The Dream Maker* started, and Jordan turned to watch as Derek and Tyler popped up from the cabin. Tyler moved to untie the boat.

"Tyler!" Jordan yelled. Tyler and Derek both looked at him, and Mr Paxton walked out of the engine cabin. Jordan's throat almost closed up, but he gathered his courage. "Mr Paxton, I need to talk to you!"

Mr Paxton looked irritated, and Tyler and Derek rolled their eyes at each other. Jordan tried to calm the butterflies in his stomach.

"Well, this boat is leaving right now, so if you want to talk, you better climb on board. But this time, maybe try not to be so clumsy," Mr Paxton said, smiling. Jordan noticed his smile didn't reach his eyes.

Jordan was torn. He wanted to get this over with but didn't want to be stuck on their boat.

Then he remembered that his grandpa had also said that the job of people was to take care of the ocean. And, clearly, Mr Paxton did anything but that.

So Jordan squared his shoulders and hopped on the boat. Tyler untied the rope and – just as Jordan snapped on his life jacket – Mr Paxton pushed the throttle hard. The boat jumped forwards.

For the second time in two days, Jordan had to hold on tight and try to keep his food down. When the boat finally slowed, Jordan had to swallow several times to calm his rolling stomach.

The engine purred in the background as Mr Paxton came out of the engine cabin and looked through a pair of binoculars. Without saying anything, Tyler and Derek took places at starboard and port to look over the sea.

Jordan knew they were looking for Tia. He had to say something.

He cleared his throat. He started, "It . . . was wrong," he mumbled.

"Mm-hmm. That's okay, Jordan," Mr Paxton said distractedly. "We're going to try again today."

Jordan cleared his throat again. "What you're doing is wrong, Mr Paxton!" he said, louder than he intended.

Mr Paxton put down the binoculars and narrowed his eyes. He smirked. "Ahh. So your grandpa got to you, huh? Well, I don't have time for that old-fashioned nonsense. I take what I want, when I want it," he said, putting the binoculars up to his eyes again.

Tyler sniggered.

"You're a weirdo, just like your grandpa," Derek said under his breath.

Anger coursed through Jordan.

"Captain Joe is the best grandpa and the best boat captain, and he knows more about this ocean than anyone. He says our job is to protect it, not ruin it!" Jordan realized he was yelling, but he didn't care.

Before anyone could respond, Tyler yelled, "Dad! Starboard!"

Jordan's stomach sank. That could only mean Tia. He looked starboard and, sure enough, there was Tia, skimming the water. For the first time since being on the boat, though, Jordan noticed how much rougher the waves were getting. The sky had darkened even more, taking on an evil greyish-green colour. The water started to buck the boat up and down.

The next few things happened so fast, Jordan could barely process them. Mr Paxton whooped with glee and dropped the binoculars. Then he lunged for his harpoon gun at the same time as Jordan. They both got hold of it.

At the exact same moment, Tyler yelled, "DAD! It's not alone!"

The fear in Tyler's voice made Jordan turn toward Tia. Mr Paxton did too. Then they both dropped the harpoon.

Tia swam around something churning in the water. Something so big, it made a large, swirling whirlpool. As Jordan watched, a huge tentacle – easily longer than two football pitches – shot out of the water. Then another. Then another.

Then a great, big, orange eye surfaced and looked straight at Jordan.

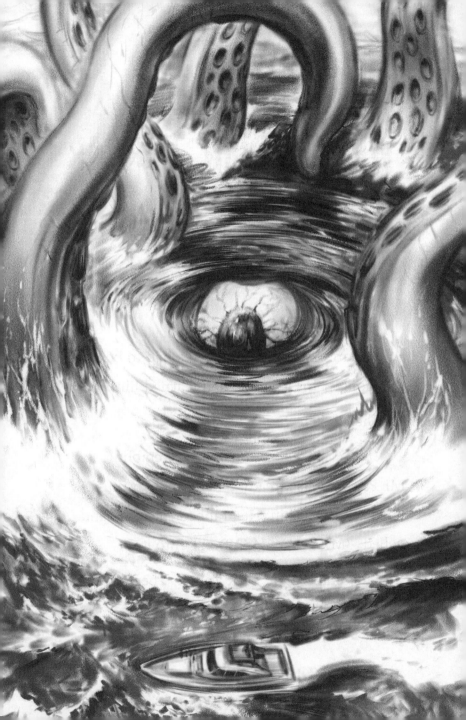

Chapter 6

WRAPPED IN TERROR

Jordan's knees buckled. This had to be the sea monster his grandpa had warned him about.

The Kraken.

"Dad?" Derek said, his voice trembling. But Mr Paxton was already moving. He sprinted to the engine cabin. He grabbed the radio and yelled, "MAYDAY, MAYDAY" into it.

Only static came back at him. Then a string of garbled words.

Finally, their parents said good night and climbed into their tents. Kaci and Abby pretended they wanted to go to sleep too. But inside their tent, they stuffed clothes in their sleeping bags to make vaguely human shapes. Then they took their torches and walked down the trail. They found a place to sit behind some bushes that gave them a view of the tent.

Kaci scratched her arm and suddenly realized something. She sat up straight and grabbed Abby's arm.

"Wait. Our arms," Kaci whispered. "Our marks have returned. What if they are tracking devices or something?"

Abby thought for a moment and then tapped her torch. "These torches have pretty strong magnets in their handles. We could rub them over our arms in case the devices are magnetised."

Kaci shrugged. She knew magnets could scramble computer hard drives, but she felt pretty silly rubbing a torch on her arm. Still, she trusted that Abby knew what she was doing. As she thought that, her gut twisted again. She took a deep breath and grabbed Abby's hand.

"Abby," Kaci started, then let go of her hand. She looked down, but then made herself look Abby in the eyes. "I'm really sorry. I should have stopped people from picking on you. I watched it happen and I didn't do anything. I will from now on."

Abby looked down. Kaci couldn't see her face very clearly in the dim moonlight, but when Abby looked up, she saw the flash of her teeth. She was smiling.

"I would like that," Abby replied. Then she giggled. "I'm sorry too. I thought you were kind of ditzy or something. But it turns out you're really not."

Kaci grinned. "Well, I just rubbed a torch on my arm, so maybe you weren't totally wrong."

They settled in and waited. Kaci felt like a weight had been lifted off her shoulders. Even if she was being hunted by aliens, at least she could finally feel good about herself. She'd finally done the right thing. Or at least started along that path. She would try to remember this feeling.

With the night breeze on her cheeks, Kaci's muscles relaxed, and she started drifting off.

Suddenly, something poked her hard, and Kaci sat up with a start. Somehow, she had fallen asleep. She rubbed her eyes and turned to Abby, who sat next to her, on alert. Her eyes were wide in the bright white light shining from their campground.

Light. In their campground. While it was night.

Kaci followed Abby's line of sight and saw where the light came from. A bright beam shone down right where their tent used to be. But as Kaci followed the light up, she saw their tent float up into a large, hovering ship above them.

"Oh. My. Gosh," she whispered.

Abby looked at her. "We should warn our parents."

Kaci nodded. But before they could run to the campground, the tent crashed back down. Then another beam of light split the night. This one searched around the campsite, clearly looking for Kaci and Abby.

Abby looked at Kaci. "RUN," she whispered fiercely.

Kaci didn't have to be told twice.

Chapter 7

THE GLOWING MARK

The girls crashed through the forest, running as fast as they could. Kaci felt like every tree root and vine reached up to grab her feet, tripping her. She could hear Abby panting ahead of her.

The light from behind them blinked off suddenly and now they were in darkness again, lit only by the moon. Kaci realized she'd dropped her torch somewhere. Still, Abby crashed through the undergrowth of the forest ahead of her. Kaci wasn't sure where they were running – just that they were running away. But suddenly, Kaci could make out the clearing and its circle of trees in the moonlight.

Kaci tried to grab Abby's arm –if the clearing was a UFO site, this was the last place they wanted to be. But their momentum propelled them into the clearing. Abby stopped, and Kaci turned round. She was about to run the other way when Abby pointed to something with a trembling finger. Kaci looked, following the direction of her finger.

The mark on the tree glowed.

But more importantly, the marks on their forearms glowed too.

Suddenly, a white beam shot down, trapping Kaci and Abby. Kaci's feet left the ground. Out of the corner of her eye, she saw the same thing happen to Abby. They floated – suspended just inches above the ground – unable to move.

Out of the darkness around them, two very tall, grey aliens walked up to them. Huge, black eyes took up most of the space on their large, bulbous heads. Their mouths were tiny and they only had slits where a nose on a human would be. Kaci wanted to scream, but her mouth wouldn't move. The scream stuck in her throat.

"Experiment K and Experiment A seem to have found a way to temporarily disable our trackers," one of the aliens said.

"We cannot lose these experiments," said the other alien. "This is a long-term study. These are fairly new humans and we need all the data we can get."

Kaci desperately tried to move. Though it took a monumental effort, she felt her hand move just a little towards Abby.

"We will have to instal more permanent trackers. Perhaps in a place where their eye orbs cannot detect them," said the first alien.

"A more extensive procedure, yes," said the other alien thoughtfully.

Kaci moved her arm a little more. The words she'd said to Abby earlier rang in her head. The aliens may have taken each girl individually before, but now Kaci and Abby had each other. And there was hope in that.

"If we are to experiment on them their whole lives, we cannot allow them to know about it in any way," said the first alien. "In our other experiments, humans who remembered – what is that Earth saying? Oh yes, 'lost their minds'. We must not let that happen with these two promising subjects."

The aliens turned towards each other and seemed to be ignoring Kaci and Abby. Kaci used all her strength to move her hand over more. Though she couldn't see her face, Kaci knew Abby was trying too. Their hands inched closer and closer.

"Where shall we implant the tracker? Behind their eye sockets? Deep in their nose canals?" one of the aliens was saying.

Suddenly, Kaci's hand met Abby's. The force field around them rippled, and the girls silently dropped the few inches to the ground. The pull of the light beam was gone.

Still holding hands, and without speaking, the girls slowly backed away. If they could just get to the edge of the forest, they might be able to lose the aliens and disable their marks again.

Step by step, Kaci and Abby edged further and further from the two aliens. Then, when they reached the edge of the light beam, they both twisted round and began running.

Kaci could see the trees right in front of her. She made it to the edge of the forest and almost jumped for joy. But then something caught her again. She watched in horror as she and Abby were trapped in separate beams— beams that moved them straight back to the aliens.

If Kaci could have moved, she would have cried.

One of the aliens walked up to Kaci and cupped her face, almost gently. Kaci wanted to bite its grey, bony fingers, but she couldn't even turn her head.

"Silly humans," said the alien, its tiny mouth bending into a thin smile. "You must not run. Your participation in our experiment is a lifelong *honour*. But do not worry. From this moment on you will only remember us when we come for you. After all, those are the best times to study your fear."

Kaci wanted desperately to yell back an answer. She wanted desperately to say she didn't want any of this to happen.

But instead of screaming at the terrible alien in front of her, Kaci watched as the alien next to Abby snapped its bony fingers. Then Kaci blacked out.

Chapter 8

A GREAT HOLIDAY AFTER ALL

When Kaci woke up in the morning, she
didn't feel very rested. She also felt like she was
forgetting something, but she didn't know what.
Even weirder, her head hurt and a spot behind
her right ear throbbed slightly for some reason.
She rubbed it but couldn't feel any bug bites or
obvious sores.

Kaci yawned and looked at Abby sleeping
across from her. Had they talked last night?

Kaci knew she should apologize to Abby for letting people pick on her. She still had to do that. She'd meant to last night, but all she could remember was eating her dinner. She didn't even remember falling asleep in the tent.

Just then, Abby woke up. She sat up and rubbed her head, then her eyes.

"My head," she groaned, swallowing.

"My head hurts too," Kaci said. "And behind my right ear for some reason."

Abby felt behind her ear. "Mine does too," she said. "What happened last night?"

Kaci shook her head. "I don't know. Maybe one too many s'mores?"

Abby smiled and then grimaced. "Yeah, maybe."

Kaci stretched again. "Oh well. I'm going to grab some painkillers. Do you need some?"

Abby nodded. "Definitely."

Kaci stood up but stopped. "Hey, Abby," she said. Abby looked at her with squinty eyes.

"Yeah?" she said, still rubbing her forehead.

"I didn't really want to come on this holiday," she said. "I thought it would be pretty boring. And . . . well, I didn't really know you. But it turned out to be a great holiday after all. I'm glad I came."

Abby smiled again. "Me too." She looked thoughtful for a minute. "Though I'm having trouble remembering what we've done this whole time."

Kaci smiled at Abby. "It'll come back to us eventually, I'm sure," she said.

Just as Kaci was about to leave the tent, Abby's face went slack and her eyes glossed over. Kaci spotted something red glowing

behind Abby's ear, and the memories of the night before suddenly flooded back.

As pain flared behind Kaci's own right ear, fear engulfed her body. Just before she blacked out, she knew one thing for certain.

The aliens wanted them back.

ABOUT THE AUTHOR

Megan Atwood is a writer and professor with more than forty-five published books. She lives in New Jersey, USA, where she wrangles cats, dreams up scary stories and thinks of ways to keep kids on the edge of their seats.

ABOUT THE ILLUSTRATOR

Neil Evans is a Welsh illustrator. A lifelong comic art fan, he drifted into children's illustration at art college and has since done plenty of both. He enjoyed a few years as a member of various unheard-of indie rock bands (and as a maker of bizarre small press comics), before settling down to get serious about making a living from illustration. He loves depicting emotion, expression and body language, and he loves inventing unusual creatures and places. When not hunched over a graphics tablet, he can usually be found hunched over a guitar or dreaming up book pitches and silly songs with his partner, Susannah. They live together in North Wales.

GLOSSARY

animatronic having to do with robots that appear lifelike

choker necklace that fits closely around the neck

disable take away the ability to do something

encounter unexpected or difficult meeting

oasis place in a desert where there is water for plants, animals and people

orb spherical object such as a globe or an eyeball

permanent lasting for a long time or forever

posture position of your body

Sasquatch hairy, humanoid creature of legend; also known as Bigfoot

supernatural something that cannot be given an ordinary, rational explanation

TALK ABOUT IT

1. Abby gets judged and bullied at school for the way she dresses and the types of things she is interested in. Has anyone ever judged you before they got to know you? How did that make you feel?

2. Kaci and Abby decide to hide in the woods to see if the aliens come for them at night. Do you think they made the right choice? What do you think would have happened if they had stayed in their tent?

3. One of the aliens says that Kaci and Abby's participation in their study is an honour. Why do you think the alien said that?

WRITE ABOUT IT

1. This story features grey aliens, who are known for their grey skin, bulbous heads and large, black eyes. If you could create your own alien for this story, what would it look like? Write a paragraph describing your alien and draw a picture of it.

2. Both Kaci and Abby experience time-lapses where they can't remember what happened during several hours of their life. Pick one of the two characters and write a scene describing what happened during her time-lapse.

3. At the end of the story, Kaci knows the aliens are coming back for them. Write a new chapter to show what happens next. Do they take Kaci and Abby onto their ship or into outer space? You decide!